ANIMALS of the SNOW and ICE

Polar Bears

Hunters of the Snow and Ice

Elaine Landau

Contents

Words to Know 3
Animals of the Snow and Ice 4
All About Polar Bears 9
Super Swimmers! 10
The Polar Bear's Home 12
Built for Arctic Life 15
What's for Dinner? 16
Is It Mating Season? 19
Here Come the Cubs 20
Polar Bears in Trouble 24
Save Those Bears! 27
Fun Facts About Polar Bears 28
Learn More: Books and Web Sites .. 30
Index 31

Words to Know

Arctic—The large frozen area around the North Pole.

global warming—A rise in Earth's average temperature. This warming causes climate change.

greenhouse gases—Some gases in the air, such as carbon dioxide and methane, that trap Earth's heat.

predator—A person or animal that hunts and kills other animals for food.

prey—An animal that is hunted to be eaten.

threatened—A kind of animal that is in danger of disappearing from Earth forever.

Animals of the Snow and Ice

You are near the North Pole. The temperature is less than 50 degrees below zero Fahrenheit. The wind is strong enough to knock you over. It has been snowing for days.

You see something large in the distance. It looks like a giant in a fluffy white suit. You soon see that it is an animal. You have spotted a polar bear.

From a distance, people thought polar bears looked like old men in cloaks!

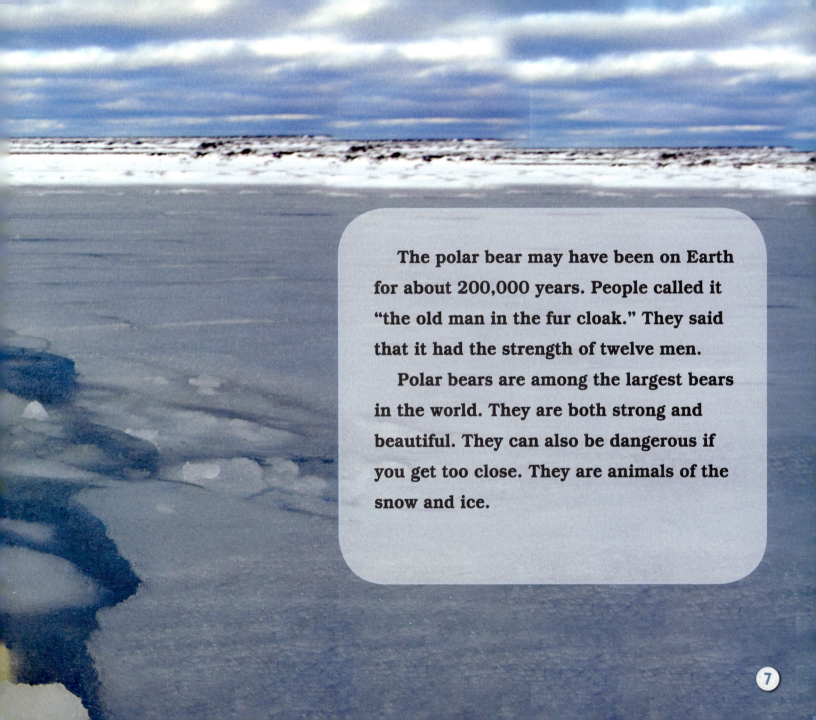

The polar bear may have been on Earth for about 200,000 years. People called it "the old man in the fur cloak." They said that it had the strength of twelve men.

Polar bears are among the largest bears in the world. They are both strong and beautiful. They can also be dangerous if you get too close. They are animals of the snow and ice.

This is what polar bear hair looks like under a microscope. Notice how it is hollow in the middle.

On his hind legs, a polar bear is taller than a tall man.

All About Polar Bears

Polar bears are bigger than people. A tall man is about six feet tall. A male polar bear is about eight to ten feet long. Male polar bears are at least two (and sometimes three!) times bigger than females.

Male polar bears weigh between 780 and 1,500 pounds. That is about as much as seven adult men. Females weigh between 330 and 550 pounds.

A polar bear's fur may look white. Yet each hair is really a clear, hollow tube. The tubes have no color, but reflect the white light of the sun. This makes the bear look white.

Under its fur, a polar bear's skin is black! Yet you never see this. A polar bear is almost fully covered with fur.

Super Swimmers!

Polar bears are sometimes called sea bears. These bears are strong swimmers. They can swim for hours. Some have swum over sixty miles without stopping.

Polar bears are also fast swimmers. They can swim at a rate of six miles per hour. The fastest humans can only swim about five miles per hour, but most humans swim about a half-mile per hour.

These bears are built to swim. Their large paws help push them through the water. Their back feet and legs act as rudders. Polar bears swim with their eyes open and their nostrils shut.

Polar bears are great swimmers, and they

The Polar Bear's Home

Polar bears are found in most areas of the north, where the sea is covered in ice nearly all year. This region is known as the Arctic. The bears prefer to live on sea ice near the shore. They also like to have openings in the ice so they can easily get to the water.

Parts of five countries lie within this area. They are called the "polar bear nations." The United States (Alaska) and Canada are two of these countries. Greenland, Russia, and Norway are the others.

Polar bears do not stay in just one place. They roam over a large area in search of food. A bear's home range may be in more than one country. Some even travel as far north as the North Pole. However, this is not very common, because the bears cannot find as much food there.

The five "polar bear nations" are the United States, Canada, Greenland, Russia, and Norway.

Polar bears prefer to live in places where they are close to the sea, so they can hunt more easily.

A polar bear's light-colored coat helps it blend in with its environment and keeps it safe.

Built for Arctic Life

Polar bears are well-suited for the Arctic. Their black skin helps protect them from very strong sunlight in the summer. Their fur coats are heavier than those of other bears. Underneath, they have a thick, wooly undercoat. Polar bears also have a layer of fat to keep them warm. This layer may be from two to four inches thick.

These bears have large, sturdy legs and big paws. Their paws act like snowshoes. They help the bears balance their weight on the snow and ice.

The polar bear's light-colored fur is also useful in the Arctic. The bears blend in well with the snow and ice. It is hard for hunters to spot them.

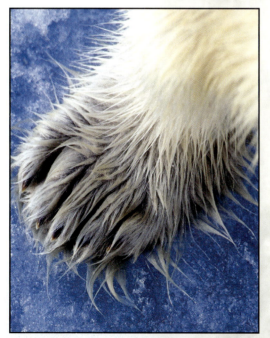

A polar bear's paw

What's for Dinner?

The polar bear's main food is ringed seal. A bear will wait on the ice near a seal's breathing hole. When the seal comes up for air, the bear kills it. Often the seal does not see the bear until it is too late.

Polar bears also attack seals that are resting on the ice. They sneak up and strike the seal before it can get back into the water. The bear kills the seal with a powerful swing of its paw or a bite to the head.

Birds and small reindeer have been prey for polar bears as well. The bears also feed on walruses and beached whales that have died. At times, polar bears eat grasses, seaweed, and berries, too. But the food from the ocean is most important for the bears.

Polar bears kill seals with a swipe of the paw or a bite to the head.

Is It Mating Season?

Most polar bears live alone. They come together to mate in March, April, and May. Females mate when they are four or five years old. Males mate when they are from five to ten years old.

A male bear may mate with a few females. After mating, the female gets ready for the birth of her young. This will happen in about eight months.

In October and November, females that are going to have cubs dig small dens. The dens are made of snow and ice. It will be about forty degrees warmer inside the den than outside.

The female spends the winter there. Her cubs are born in December or January. The other polar bears stay on the sea ice to hunt seals during the winter.

Here Come the Cubs

Polar bears usually give birth to two cubs. Rarely, there may be three cubs, and often there is just one cub.

The babies are only about twelve inches long when they are born. They weigh about a pound. That is much less than a human newborn. A polar bear mother can easily hold a cub in her paw.

These newborns cannot see, hear, or walk. Their fur is so thin that they look almost hairless. The cubs stay close to their mother for warmth. They drink her milk.

By March or April, the cubs have grown big enough to leave the den. Soon their mother will bring them to the sea ice. They learn to hunt by watching her. When they are about two and a half years old, the cubs and their mother part. Now the young bears are on their own.

Polar Bears in Trouble

People are the polar bear's only predator. For thousands of years, the people who live near the bears have hunted them. Today they sell polar bear skins. This helps them make money.

In the past, some polar bear populations were hunted too much. Today, hunting is managed well. It is not a threat to most polar bears.

However, global warming is big threat to these bears. Much of the sea ice on which they live is melting. This makes it harder for polar bears to hunt seals. Some bears have starved. Others have drowned trying to reach sea ice. Without sea ice, polar bears cannot catch their food.

Today there are 20,000 to 25,000 polar bears in the world. Many of these bears will die if something is not done to reduce the amount of greenhouse gases people put into the air. These gases trap Earth's heat. Large amounts of greenhouse gases make the world warmer. A warmer world will have less sea ice for the polar bears.

Save Those Bears!

Help may be on the way! Some countries have passed new laws to protect the places where polar bears live. Laws have also been passed to limit the hunting of polar bears. In May 2008, the United States listed polar bears as threatened. This means that the polar bear is in danger of dying out, and more laws will protect it.

Scientists are also looking for ways for people to use less gas and coal. This will lessen greenhouse gases, which will reduce global warming.

Polar bears are rare and special animals. People have always admired their strength and beauty, but now these bears need our help. Polar bears have a right to their place on the planet. We must make sure they are not robbed of it.

Fun Facts About Polar Bears

- Polar bears are good divers. They can stay underwater for as long as two minutes.
- The oldest known polar bear in the wild lived for 32 years. The oldest known polar bear in a zoo lived for 41 years.
- Polar bears have fur on the bottoms of their paws. It keeps them from slipping on the ice.
- A polar bear can run as fast as 25 miles per hour for short distances.
- Polar bears can smell a seal out of water up to 20 miles away.
- In 1979, three polar bears at the San Diego Zoo turned green! Green algae had grown in their hollow hair tubes.

Learn More

Books

Cherry, Lynne, and Gary Braasch. *How We Know What We Know About Our Changing Climate: Scientists and Kids Explore Global Warming.* Nevada City, Calif.: Dawn Publications, 2008.

Hirschi, Ron. *Our Three Bears.* Honesdale, Pa.: Boyds Mill Press, 2008.

Rosing, Norbert, and Elizabeth Carney. *Face to Face with Polar Bears.* Washington, D.C.: National Geographic, 2007.

Squire, Ann O. *Polar Bears.* New York: Children's Press, 2007.

Web Sites

Children's Really Wild Zone—Amazing Animals. *Polar Bears.* <http://www.bbc.co.uk/nature/reallywild/amazing/polar_bear.shtml>

Polar Bear Nation's Adventure Learning Program. <http://polarbearnation.com/alp>

Index

A

Arctic, 12

C

Canada, 12
cubs, 19, 20, 22

D

den, 19, 22

F

fat, 15
food, 12, 16, 25
fur, 9, 16

G

global warming, 25, 27
greenhouse gases, 25, 27
Greenland, 12

L

legs, 10, 15

M

mating, 19

N

North Pole, 4, 12
Norway, 12

P

paws, 10, 15, 20
polar bear
    conservation, 27
    height, 9
    hunting of, 24
    nations, 12
    population size, 25
    range, 12
    weight, 9
predator, 24
prey, 16

R

Russia, 12

S

sea bear, 10
sea ice, 22, 25
seal, 16, 19, 25
skin, 9, 24
swimming, 10

T

threatened, 27

U

United States, 12, 27

W

walrus, 16
whale, 16

Enslow Elementary, an imprint of Enslow Publishers, Inc.
Enslow Elementary® is a registered trademark of Enslow Publishers, Inc.

Copyright © 2010 by Elaine Landau

All rights reserved.

No part of this book may be reproduced by any means
without the written permission of the publisher.

Library of Congress Cataloging-in-Publication Data

Landau, Elaine.
  Polar bears : hunters of the snow and ice / Elaine Landau.
    p. cm. — (Animals of the snow and ice)
  Includes bibliographical references and index.
  Summary: "Provides information for young readers about polar bears, including habitat, eating habits, mating, babies, and conservation"—Provided by publisher.
  ISBN 978-0-7660-3461-7
  1. Polar bear—Juvenile literature. I. Title.
  QL737.C27L32 2011
  599.786—dc22
                                                            2009006481

Printed in the United States of America

092009 Lake Book Manufacturing, Inc., Melrose Park, IL

10 9 8 7 6 5 4 3 2 1

To Our Readers: We have done our best to make sure all Internet addresses in this book were active and appropriate when we went to press. However, the author and the publisher have no control over and assume no liability for the material available on those Internet sites or on other Web sites they may link to. Any comments or suggestions can be sent by e-mail to comments@enslow.com or to the address on the back cover.

 Enslow Publishers, Inc., is committed to printing our books on recycled paper. The paper in every book contains 10% to 30% post-consumer waste (PCW). The cover board on the outside of each book contains 100% PCW. Our goal is to do our part to help young people and the environment too!

Every effort has been made to locate all copyright holders of material used in this book. If any errors or omissions have occurred, corrections will be made in future editions of this book.

Photo Credits: © 1999, Artville, LLC, p. 12; © 2009 Jupiterimages Corporation, pp. 2, 5, 32; Andrew Syred / Photo Researchers, Inc., p. 8; Dan Guravich / Photo Researchers, Inc., p. 18; © David Parsons/iStockphoto.com p. 1; © David Pike/naturepl.com, pp. 22–23; © Fritz Polking/Visuals Unlimited, Inc., p. 21; © Gerald & Buff Corsi/Visuals Unlimited, Inc., p. 15; © John Pitcher/iStockphoto.com, p. 3; © Mark Newman/Alaskastock, p. 29; © Martha Holmes/naturepl.com, p. 11; © Matthias Breiter/Minden Pictures, p. 14; © Rinie Van Meurs/Foto Natura/Minden Pictures, pp. 13, 17; © Steven Kazlowski/Alaskastock, pp. 6, 8, 24–25; © iStockphoto.com/John Pitcher, p. 30; © Thomas Mangelsen/Minden Pictures, p. 26.

Cover Photo: © Michio Hoshino/Minden Pictures

Enslow Elementary
an imprint of
Enslow Publishers, Inc.
40 Industrial Road
Box 398
Berkeley Heights, NJ 07922
USA
http://www.enslow.com